Enchanted Collar™ #2

S0-APM-058

Dog Fight

by Robin Y. Yang

Find color illustrations, previews, videos, toys, worksheets, and parenting tips on the Web at www.EnchantedCollar.com

Like us on Facebook at www.facebook.com/EnchantedCollar

Enchanted Collar™ **books:**

A Strange Gift (#1)
Dog Fight (#2)
Paradise Lost (#3)
Squirrel Pot Pie (#4)
Bandits and Robbers (#5)
Shark Attack (#6)

Here's what kids have say to Robin Yang, author of the Enchanted Collar™ series:

I love Earl. He is funny. I love Skipper too. He is so nice. I think he is shy.
— **Ava L., age 6, Connecticut**

I liked the book a lot, especially the pictures. I want to know what happens to Eli on his journey. I hope you write more soon so I can enjoy reading more about his story.
— **Brian G., age 7, New Jersey**

I liked this book as much as I like puppies, and I really love puppies! When I read Eli went out on his own and he couldn't read or write, I felt kind of sad and scared. Then I read about Earl, and I laughed because he was really funny!
— **Athena S., age 7, New York**

The stories were fun. I loved them. I keep telling my daddy I want a puppy; I tell him I wish I had a puppy like Eli.
— **Grace L., age 8, Connecticut**

I like the story and the characters. Earl is very funny, especially when he eats Eli's food. After all, he is a pig! When can I read the next book?
— **Jake R., age 9, Florida**

It's a very entertaining story. If I were Eli, I would have saved my money.
— **Sienna S., age 9, New York**

This was a really good book. I liked the words you used in the story. The words actually formed pictures in my head! I learned not to spend all of my money on one thing and to make my money to last a year or so. This story taught me a very good lesson.

— **Nathan X., age 11, Colorado**

This is a really great series of books! I like the fast-paced plot lines.

— **Taylor G., age 12, Connecticut**

I loved your story because it was cute. I could actually imagine what Eli, Earl, William, and all of the other characters looked like in my mind. I liked the fact that Eli never breaks his promises. Eli was very brave to accept such a dangerous quest and journey at such a young age. His story in Book 2 has taught me not to be greedy. I've learned that you should know how much something costs before you buy it and make sure you have enough money to pay. I am very eager to read the next book in the series.

— **Carol X., age 14, Colorado**

What teachers, parents, and financial experts say:

This book is an absolute gem. It entertains with a brisk tempo and reminds readers of the importance of financial literacy. Eli's journey is a page turner.
— **Kabir Seghal, investment banker and author of *Walk in My Shoes* and *Jazzocracy***

I like the way Robin Yang's book weaves important financial precepts into an imaginative story that my children enjoyed reading. This establishes a basis for them to eventually learn the "mechanics" of money management.
— **Peter Lannigan, investment strategist, portfolio manager, and homeschooling father of two**

Robin Yang's book is a wonderful way to lead young children toward a successful financial future. Full of interesting and innovative ideas about budgeting, saving, banking, and investing, the Enchanted Collar™ series is a helpful and fun tool for teachers as well as students. Robin Yang should be congratulated for creating such an interesting method to teach kids about money.
— **Don Elliott, retired superintendent, Arkansas Public Schools**

Financial literacy, like literacy in general, should be acquired young. As a father as well as an economist, I look forward to my young son being able to read Robin Yang's imaginative and educational Enchanted Collar™ books.
— **Benn Steil, Ph.D., Director of International Economics for the Council on Foreign Relations and coauthor of**

Dog
Fight

For my mom and dad, who taught me priceless life lessons, and
for my big brother, who raised me and protected me

ISBN: 1466407816
ISBN-13: 9781466407817

Library of Congress Control Number: 2011918217
CreateSpace, North Charleston, South Carolina

TABLE OF CONTENTS

CHAPTER 1

Books in a Ditch

Bam! A pink bundle fell off the truck as it climbed the steep hill. The bundle rolled toward Eli like a soccer ball. A scream came out of the bundle.

"*Oink...* Help!"

Eli rushed forward, trying to catch the bundle. But it was bigger and heavier than he was. He was knocked over and rolled with the bundle into a ditch.

"Ouch!" Eli winced as he scrambled to his feet. He craned his neck and looked down at his own back. Thank goodness, there was no sign of blood. He shook his head, wagged his tail, and jiggled his body. Dry leaves and grass fell off. He blinked several times and noticed something odd: books were scattered everywhere!

"*Oink*. Pardon me!" A little pig squeezed past Eli in the narrow ditch. He picked up a book and put it in his backpack. As if he just remembered something important, he turned around and looked at Eli.

"Are you alright?" he asked.

"Yeah…" Eli was not exactly sure. No wonder the little pig had knocked him over. All those books in his backpack had to weigh a ton! Eli stared into the eyes of the smiling little pig. "Who are you?"

"Oh, dear, where are my manners?" The pig was flustered. He extended his hand to Eli. "My name is Earl. What's your name?"

"Eli." Eli shook hands with Earl. "What do you do with these books?"

"I read them," Earl said, somewhat indignantly, as if the answer should have been obvious to Eli.

"You know how to read?" Eli asked with surprise. "How did you learn that?"

"My friend Charlene taught me. She is…excuse me…she *was* a spider."

Eli picked up a book. He wished he had a spider to teach him how to read. He flipped through the pages but did not see any pictures. "Here," he said as he gave the book back to Earl.

"Thank you." Earl took the book, put it in his backpack, and closed the flap. "I guess I have all of my books back."

"What are you doing here?" Eli asked. "How did you fall off the truck?"

"I didn't fall." Earl's voice trailed into a murmur. "I jumped."

"You jumped?" Eli looked at Earl's short, chubby legs. This little pig must be out of his mind. "Why?"

"Because I don't want to die." Earl's lips quivered. Two shiny tears rolled down his cheeks.

"I am sorry." Eli did not mean to upset Earl. He tried to put his arm around Earl's shoulders to comfort him, but Earl's body was so broad that Eli's arm could not reach around him. So he patted Earl's back gently instead. "There, there…"

Eli was still confused. Nothing Earl said made any sense. He waited until

Earl's tears had stopped and asked softly, "How is jumping off a running truck going to help you? Where are your mom and dad?"

"Wooaaa..." Earl's sob turned into a full-scale bawl.

"Sorry! Sorry!" Eli apologized frantically. *What did I say? What have I done? What's wrong with this pig?* he wondered. Eli was lost. Other than sitting beside Earl in the ditch and watching him cry, he did not know what else to do.

After what seemed like hours, Earl's torrent of tears slowed to a trickle. He wiped his nose with the backs of his hands. "Mom... Dad...," Earl sniffled. "They have been taken to the slaughterhouse."

Slaughterhouse? Eli recalled the truck full of squealing pigs.

"I thought we were going out for ice cream. But then I found out from other pigs where the truck was really taking us," Earl continued, "so I jumped."

"Wow!" Eli gasped. "You are really brave!"

"Really?" Earl stopped crying. "You really think so?" He was rarely praised for bravery. "I figured I would rather die in one piece than become pork chops."

"No, you are not going to die!" Eli proclaimed. "You will live to one hundred years old!"

"I will?" Earl wiped his tears away. His eyes twinkled with hope.

"Yes!" Eli said with all the certainty in the world. "You and I are going to climb out of this ditch. We will go on adventures. We will meet exciting people. We will taste all sorts of exotic food."

"Food!" Earl's eyes sparkled. "OK. Let's get out of here!" He put his hands on the wall of the ditch and was ready to climb out. The wall rose above his head. All he could see was a sliver of the evening sky above the ditch.

Like a balloon punctured by a needle, Earl slumped to the ground. "Forget it," he said, resigned. "We are too far down. We will never be able to get out of this ditch."

CHAPTER
2

Sorry! Sorry!

"Yes, we will!" Eli said determinedly. "You can step on my shoulders. With your height and mine together, we should be able to reach the top."

Eli squatted down. Earl stepped onto his shoulders and reached up, but he still could not touch the edge of the ditch.

"A little higher, please," Earl urged.

Eli struggled to stand up. Earl wobbled on top of him. Before Eli could straighten his back, his legs buckled. He collapsed under Earl's weight.

Earl tumbled over and fell on his bottom. "It won't work." He was about to cry again.

Eli stopped him before tears had a chance to roll from his eyes. "Let's try again. I am lighter than you are. Let me stand on your shoulders this time."

Earl eyed him with suspicion. "If you get out first, are you going to forget about me?" he asked warily.

"Of course not!" Eli put his hand on Earl's shoulder reassuringly.

Earl gazed into Eli's eyes. For a few seconds, neither of them spoke. Earl weighed different options in his head. Then he softened his gaze. "OK, you can step on my shoulders," he said.

Eli climbed onto Earl's shoulders. Earl stood up. Eli's hands were just about to reach the edge of the ditch. He sprang upward, hooked onto the edge with his nails, and pulled himself out of the ditch. He immediately turned around and extended his hand to Earl. "Grab onto me. I will pull you out."

Earl reached out. His arms were so short that his fingers could not touch Eli's. As they struggled, they heard a rustling noise in the distance.

"Someone is coming!" Eli jumped up in excitement. "I will go ask for help."

"No, wait!" Earl urged in a hushed voice. "It could be the slaughterhouse people looking for me!"

"Good point!" Eli perked up his ears and listened intently. He could hear faint voices. The voices grew louder. Two people were arguing.

"You didn't tie those pigs to the truck board!" one voice shouted angrily. "It's all your fault!"

"Oh, yeah?" the other voice howled. "Who suggested we pretend to take those pigs out for ice cream, smarty pants?"

"You are right!" Eli whispered to Earl. "They are the slaughterhouse people looking for you."

"Oh!" Earl panicked. "What are we going to do?"

"Quick!" Eli pointed to a pile of dry leaves in the ditch. "You hide underneath those leaves. I will distract them."

Earl dove underneath the leaves. Eli straightened up and walked nonchalantly toward the arguing voices. As the voices got closer, Eli saw two bulldogs. One was carrying a torch. Under the flickering torchlight, they looked like demons from the underworld, their faces twisted. They stopped arguing in mid-sentence when they spotted Eli.

"Hey, you!" one bulldog called in a gruff voice. "Have you seen a little pig?"

"Yes!" Eli said cheerfully. "He asked me for the closest ice cream parlor. I told him to go that way." Eli pointed deep into the forest. The two bulldogs dashed off immediately.

Eli waited until the sound of their footsteps had disappeared and then hurried back to the ditch.

"Hey, Earl!" Eli called down. "It's OK to come out now."

Earl poked his head out of the dry leaves. One leaf was dangling from the corner of his mouth. He looked like a beat-up piñata. Eli tried to stifle a laugh but failed. He burst into a loud guffaw.

"Ha, ha." Earl spit the leaf out and stood up. "Very funny! Now get me out of here!"

Eli extended his hand. Earl shook his head. "We tried that. It doesn't work!"

Eli looked around and said, "Wait!" He disappeared from Earl's sight.

"Where are you going?" Earl asked anxiously but got no answer. "I knew I shouldn't have trusted that dog!" he spat. "What am I going to do now?"

CHAPTER 3

Seize Them!

A few minutes later, Earl heard footsteps approaching. He looked up. Eli was waving a long, thick vine at him.

"Grab onto this!" Eli threw one end of the vine down. Earl grabbed it.

"Now climb out." Eli pulled the other end. Earl braced one foot against the wall, and then the other.

"*Ahhhh…*" Eli ground his teeth as he pulled the vine. It moved one inch… then another inch…

Snap! Eli stumbled several steps back. The vine had broken into two pieces. He threw down his piece and rushed to check on Earl.

Earl was sitting at the bottom of the ditch, his hands still clutching the broken vine. His backpack hung off one shoulder. A few books peeked out from underneath the flap.

"Sorry, Eli." Earl looked up at him in total despair. "I guess I am too heavy for you."

"No," Eli replied, "it's not you, Earl! It's the books! Get rid of those books!"

Earl took off his backpack. Instead of throwing it aside, though, he hugged it to his chest. "No, I can't. These books were birthday gifts from my parents. They are the only things I have left in this world."

Earl's words reminded Eli of something of his own. Absentmindedly, he ran his finger around his neck. The collar was still there.

"OK," Eli conceded. "Keep the books. Wait here."

A few minutes later, Eli reappeared at the edge of the ditch. This time, he had two long, thick vines. He twisted them into one and threw one end down.

"Tie this to the strap of your back-pack," he said. "I will pull your books out first and then you." Earl followed his instructions.

After Eli fished the backpack out, he threw the vine back down and said, "Wrap it around your waist. Then climb with your hands and feet while I pull."

Earl complied. Eli wrapped the other end of the vine around his own waist. He leaned backward and pulled with as much force as he could muster. The vine inched upward out of the ditch. This time, it moved much faster.

Finally, Earl's head popped out of the ground, then his chest, his belly, and his legs. When Earl's whole body was out, Eli dropped to his knees, panting. Earl flopped down beside him.

"Thanks," Earl mumbled between heaving breaths.

"You are welcome." Eli smiled. "Ready for some food?"

"Yes!" Earl sprang to his feet. Eli shook his head with a laugh and handed Earl's backpack to him.

As they got to their feet, the night sky became a little lighter. A torchlight was approaching them.

"Seize them!" a voice hollered. It sounded familiar. It was one of the slaughterhouse bulldogs! Those two had come back!

"Run!" Eli shouted at Earl. Both of them bolted into the forest. Leaves brushed by Eli. Grass rustled under his feet. As he sprang ahead, he realized something was missing. He stopped and looked behind him. Where was Earl?

"Help!" Earl cried far behind him. Eli turned and ran back. In the torchlight, he saw Earl kicking and screaming. He could not break free from the bulldogs' grip.

"Let him go!" Eli bellowed.

"Oh, yeah?" one bulldog sneered. "Who do you think you are?" He let go of Earl and advanced toward Eli.

"I am Eli." His heart was pounding fast, but Eli kept his voice calm. He looked straight into the bulldog's eyes and held his gaze steady. The bulldog took a step back. Then he braced himself and laughed nervously. "Listen to this puppy. Ha, ha."

"I am not just a puppy," Eli said sternly. He held his ground and tensed up his neck hair. "I am Eli. Let my friend go."

"Teach him a lesson, Trent!" the other bulldog yelled.

Trent stepped closer to Eli. Eli did not move. Trent cracked his knuckles. Eli did not flinch.

Whoosh! A fist swung through the air. A punch was thrown.

"Ahhhh!" A cry of pain pierced the night sky.

CHAPTER
4

Are We There Yet?

Everyone froze. Trent hopped around, shaking his right hand. It was bleeding profusely. Eli stood, unscratched. He looked down at his collar. It had spiked up.

"You brat!" The other bulldog let go of Earl and charged at Eli. He snarled a hiss, sprang high in the air, and hurled his whole body at Eli. Earl covered his eyes. He could not bear to see Eli get hurt.

"Ouch! Ouch! Ouch!"

Earl opened his eyes. The bulldog had bounced off Eli like a basketball. He was holding his back in pain.

"You will pay for this!" the two bulldogs shrieked at Eli. They scrambled to their feet and ran away.

"Wow!" Earl came up to Eli. "That's so cool!" He reached out to touch Eli's collar, but Eli blocked his hand in mid-air.

"Don't touch it," Eli warned. "You will get hurt." Eli ran his own fingers along the collar. The spikes had disappeared. The collar was smooth again.

Earl's jaw dropped. "What is this?"

"It's just my collar," Eli said, nonchalantly. "Let's go.

"Go where?" Earl asked. He still could not peel his eyes from Eli's collar.

Yeah… Go where? Eli looked around. Night had fallen. The forest, the road, everywhere he looked was dark, except for a few fireflies that flickered around them. Eli listened. No voices. No footsteps. No one was around except Earl and him.

Eli took off his collar, held it up high, and said, "Heaven, earth, show me the way." The collar sparkled and then beamed a bright path in front of Eli. He turned to Earl. "OK, we will go this way." He pointed at the lighted path. Earl did not move. He was too dumb-founded to respond.

"Heaven, earth," Eli recited to the collar, "hide your light." The light went out. Eli put the collar back around his neck and nudged Earl. "Let's go."

Earl followed Eli obediently but now could not keep his mouth shut. "What is that thing around your neck? Where did you get it? Can I get one just like that? Where exactly are we going? Where is your home? Are we there yet?"

Eli kept silent. He started to wish he had not rescued this pig. He started to miss his lonesome—but peaceful and quiet—journey. Finally, he could not stand Earl's nonstop babbling any longer.

"OK!" He halted his steps and turned to Earl. "If I tell you everything, will you promise not to ask me any more questions?"

"I promise." Earl pranced toward Eli in anticipation.

Eli sat down with Earl on a rock beside the road. In a hushed voice, he told Earl everything. When he finished, Earl was silent for a long time. The night breeze gently combed through

Eli's hair. Everything was quiet. Then, something growled.

"Oops!" Earl covered his bulging belly. "I apologize," he said and then added shyly, "I am hungry."

Growl! This time, it was Eli's belly. "Me, too!" Eli laughed.

"Then let's go eat!" Earl jumped up. He took one step, then stopped and turned to Eli. "By the way, I know your collar has shown us the direction. But exactly what are we looking for?"

"I am not sure," Eli answered. "I think the collar is directing us to find the missing jewels." He rubbed the little wolf in the middle of his collar.

"We need to find ruby, silver, pearl, and ivory."

"Hey!" Earl exclaimed. A light bulb lit up in his head. "I know a restaurant in the direction your collar pointed us. It is called Ruby Fine Dining. It has the best chocolate ice cream in the country!"

Eli rolled his eyes. Ice cream again! It seemed to be the only food Earl knew. "Do they offer anything besides ice cream?"

"Yes," Earl said. "They also have great steaks, burgers, and bones!"

"Steaks! Burgers! Bones!" Eli jumped up. "Let's go!"

They ran off into the night.

CHAPTER
5

One of Each

Faint yellow lights shone through tree leaves. Fireflies? But they looked steadier than fireflies. As Eli and Earl ran toward them, they grew brighter. Eli and Earl quickened their steps. In front of them, a bustling city came into view. Streetlights dotted the sky. Houses lined the road. Eli caught a whiff of something. He wrinkled his nose. It smelled sweet and enticing. It smelled like…steak!

"There!" Eli followed the aroma. Earl followed him. They hurried through the streets. The aroma became stronger and stronger. It led them to a sprawling building. A bright red neon sign stood on its roof.

Earl looked up and read aloud, "Ruby Fine Dining. We are here!"

Earl and Eli pushed the door open and went in.

"Good evening!" A fox girl greeted them. Her long, red hair draped over her black cocktail dress, accentuating her curvy figure. She battered her long eyelashes at Eli and asked in a brassy voice, "Would you like a table for two?"

"Yes, please," Earl replied. Eli did not say anything. The fox girl had taken his breath away.

She checked her notepad and jotted down a few words. Her brown eyes were heavily made up and looked enormous. She gestured to some benches. "Please take a seat. Your table will be ready in fifteen minutes."

Eli and Earl sat down in the restaurant lobby. They looked inside. A chandelier hung from the dome ceiling. Silverware reflected the flames from candles on tables covered with white cloths. Lemur waiters in black tuxedoes and white gloves bustled between tables. Smartly dressed people streamed in and out through the lobby. They were all talking, smiling, or laughing.

Strong aromas mixed in the air. Eli heard Earl's stomach growl louder, almost as loudly as his own. Just when they could not bear the pain in their stomachs any longer, the fox girl waved at them.

"Follow me, please."

Eli and Earl stood up. The fox girl led them through narrow aisles to a small table in the farthest corner of the restaurant. She laid two cloth-bound menus on the table, said "Enjoy!" and walked away.

Eli and Earl sat down. Right behind them, a door swung open and shut constantly. Waiters went in and out, balancing large trays of food on their shoulders. Eli felt someone was watching them. He scanned the room. Across the aisle sat a cougar girl all by herself. She looked about five or six years older than Eli. She had dark, piercing eyes. Her hair curled around her face. A red, heart-shaped necklace was wrapped around her long, smooth neck. She met Eli's eyes defiantly.

"Who is she?" Eli asked Earl.

"Huh?" Earl responded, perplexed.

"There." Eli tipped his chin in the direction of the cougar girl.

Earl looked and shrugged. "I don't know. Who cares? Let's order!"

A lemur waiter magically appeared beside their table and produced a small notepad. "What would you like, sir?"

"What desserts do you have?" Earl asked.

"We have Flan de Leche, Chocolate Soufflé, Nectarine Posset…" the waiter droned on.

Earl interrupted him before he could finish. "OK, OK. Just bring me one of each. Also, bring me some chocolate ice cream."

"Certainly, sir!" The waiter turned to Eli. "And you, sir?"

"What kinds of steaks do you have?" Eli asked.

"We have sirloin, fillet mignon, rib eye, skirt, London broil, New York strip, Hibachi, tenderloin…" the waiter went on enthusiastically.

"OK." Eli cut him short. "Bring me one of each as well."

"Certainly, sir!" The waiter shut his notebook and disappeared into the kitchen.

As Eli sipped water, he felt someone's eyes on his back again. He sneaked a glance across the aisle. The cougar girl glared at him with one brow arched. It was as if she was trying to burn a hole through his head with her piercing eyes. Eli shifted in his seat uneasily.

The cougar girl snapped her fingers in the air. A black German shepherd stepped forward to her table. He wore dark sunglasses even though he was indoors and it was nighttime. His shoulders and upper arms were so bulky that they seemed about to burst through his dark business suit.

The cougar girl crooked her index finger at him. He bowed down toward her. She whispered something into his ear. The German shepherd nodded and then walked away. Despite the weight of his tall, husky body, his steps were so light that Eli did not hear any noise when he passed by their table. Meanwhile, the cougar girl never took her eyes off Eli.

What's her problem? Eli thought to himself. Before he could discuss his concerns with Earl, their waiter came back and placed a large plate of sirloin steak in front of Eli and a big bowl of chocolate sundae in front of Earl.

"Dig in!" Earl shoved a spoon into his sundae. Eli picked up his knife and fork and focused all of his attention on his steak. It smelled heavenly! As he munched and chewed, he forgot all about the cougar girl.

Before Eli and Earl finished their meals, more food showed up on their table. They ate and ate and ate. Although they had been starving an hour earlier, now their stomachs were so full that they felt like they would burst. But the lemur kept bringing them more food. Finally, Eli and Earl simply stared at the piles of plates, burping. They could eat no more.

"Ready for your check, sir?" the waiter asked cheerfully.

"Yes, please. *Burp!*" Eli covered his mouth. "Excuse me."

"Certainly, sir!" The waiter laid a slip of paper upside down on the table. "I will be back in a moment."

Eli looked at the slip. It had a long list of words and numbers but no pictures.

They did not mean anything to him. So he handed the slip to Earl.

Earl read the slip and blew a soft whistle. Then he looked up nervously.

CHAPTER 6

That's Not Enough!

"What's wrong?" Eli asked.

"It's more than a thousand dollars," Earl whispered. Sweat beaded up on his pink forehead.

"OK," Eli said. That still did not mean anything to him. He took the money pouch out of his knapsack. "Here is money."

Earl emptied the money pouch and started counting dollar bills and coins. When he finished, more beads of sweat started to drip down his cheeks. "That's not enough!"

"What do you mean?" Eli was surprised. He thought Mom had given him a lot of money.

"There's only one hundred twenty dollars and forty-five cents here," Earl answered.

"Don't you have any money?" Eli asked.

"No!" Earl blurted out. Diners at other tables looked up at him. Earl realized he had just made a scene and immediately lowered his voice. "I lived on a pig farm. They gave us plenty of food but never any money!"

"Then how did you learn to count money?" Eli asked.

"Charlene taught me," Earl answered.

"What are we going to do now?" Eli was at a loss for ideas. He always cooked at home with Mom. They never ate out at a restaurant.

"We will leave all of the money you have here on the table and pretend it is enough. When no one is watching, we will sneak out," said Earl.

"That sounds so wrong!" Eli protested.

"Do you have a better idea?" Earl asked.

"No." Eli lowered his head. He felt so ashamed.

"Ready?" Earl whispered as he peeked around. "Run!"

Eli and Earl dashed for the door. A black wall blocked their path. Eli looked up. The German shepherd towered over them with his arms crossed. Eli knew that behind those dark sunglasses, two piercing eyes were boring a hole into his head.

"Where are you going?" the German shepherd demanded in a raspy voice.

"Err…uh…," Eli stammered.

"We are going to the restroom," Earl ventured.

"Right…" Eli tried to sound as calm as he could. "We are going to the restroom."

"The restroom is that way." The German shepherd pointed back inside the restaurant.

"Right." Eli and Earl exchanged looks. They both turned on their heels. Before they could attempt another mad dash, they felt their feet lifted off the ground. The German shepherd had hauled them up by their necks.

"Let's settle your bill first, shall we?" the German shepherd snarled. His white, dagger-like teeth glistened in the chandelier's light.

As he carried Eli and Earl back into the restaurant like two little chickens, Eli saw the other diners pointing fingers at them, whispering to each other, and shaking their heads. Eli felt his face burning, as if a bonfire had just been lit underneath him.

Three people gathered around the table where they had eaten dinner: the cougar girl, the lemur waiter, and a cougar man Eli had never seen before. The cougar man was as tall as the German shepherd and also wore a dark business suit. Unlike the German shepherd, however, he was not wearing sunglasses. His steely eyes were locked on Eli.

The German shepherd dropped Eli and Earl onto the floor.

"Thank you, Lance," the cougar man said to the German shepherd.

"My pleasure, boss." Lance bowed.

Boss turned to the lemur waiter and asked, "How much do they owe, Richard?"

"Nine hundred eighty-seven dollars and sixty-five cents, sir," Richard answered.

"You will get your fair share of a tip on the full bill," Boss assured Richard. Then he turned to the cougar girl and said, "Elda, take the money out of our safe box and pay Richard the tip these two rascals owe."

"Thank you, boss!" The lemur bowed to the cougar man.

"But Papa…" the cougar girl protested. Before she could continue, Boss raised his hand. "We will discuss this later. Right now, I need to have a conversation with these two young gentlemen."

Eli felt a little better now that Boss had referred to Earl and him as "gentlemen." He straightened his back and puffed up his chest. He liked being treated as a grown-up.

Boss put his arms around Eli and Earl and said, "Let's go to my office." His tone was polite but firm, and Eli realized it was more of an order than an invitation. He and Earl had no choice but to obey. As he walked reluctantly past the cougar girl, he cast a resentful glance at her. She must have ratted out Earl and him and gotten them into this trouble. She lifted her chin at him and smirked. Eli narrowed his eyes and clenched his teeth at her.

"Elda, you can come with us," Boss said.

"With pleasure, Papa!" Elda pranced in front of them and led the way through a narrow corridor toward the back of the restaurant.

CHAPTER 7

You Must Pay

Elda pushed the door open into a small office. Eli, Earl, and Boss followed. A large, steel desk sat in the middle of the room. File cabinets lined the walls. Pictures, certificates, and plaques hung on the wall behind the desk. Boss sat down in a leather swivel chair. Elda stood beside him. She appeared to be quite at home in this office.

"Gentlemen," Boss said, "my name is Nathan Hills. I own this restaurant. This is my daughter, Elda." He tilted his head toward the cougar girl without taking his eyes off Eli and Earl. "What are your names?"

"My name is Eli, sir." Eli tried to sound as formal as Mr. Hills. He looked at Earl. Earl was so frightened that no sound came out of his mouth. Eli answered for him. "This is my friend Earl."

"Nice to meet you, Eli and Earl." Mr. Hills pronounced each word deliberately in a deep, booming voice. "First

of all, welcome to my humble establish-
ment. Second of all, you owe me quite
a bit of money. Now tell me something,
Eli and Earl: How do you plan to pay
me?"

"Mr. Hills," Eli began, "we really want
to pay you. Honest, sir. But we have
given you all the money we have."

"Right!" Earl chimed in. "We don't
have any money left."

"Oh?" Mr. Hills raised an eyebrow.
"Then why did you order so much
food? Didn't you read the menu from
right to left?"

"Huh?" Eli looked at Earl. *Read the
menu from right to left? What is he talking
about?*

As if reading Eli's thoughts, Earl whispered into his ear, "He means we should have read the prices before we ordered the food."

"But I don't know how to read," Eli whispered back. "You know how to read. You saw the menu. Did you notice the prices?"

"Yes, I read the numbers. But I was so hungry," Earl replied as he lowered his eyes meekly, "that I did not bother to add the numbers up."

"Ha, ha!" Elda burst into laughter.

"Elda!" Mr. Hills chided. Elda covered her mouth, but her whole body still trembled with uncontrollable giggles.

Mr. Hills cleared his throat. "Well, gentlemen, if you don't have any money left, then I will have to talk to your parents. Maybe they can pay for you."

"My parents?" Eli was mortified. His throat went dry. He could not speak. Mom's words rang in his ears: "Here, all of my life's savings are in this box. It is for you to buy food, clothing, and shelter while you are on your journey. It is not for you to buy toys. Please use it wisely and make it last." What would Mom think if she learned Eli had squandered all of her life savings on one meal? She would be heartbroken! No! She must not know! Mr. Hills must not talk to her!

As Eli stared down at his shoes, Earl answered in a trembling voice, "My parents have been sent to the slaughterhouse. I don't have any parents anymore."

"I am sorry," Mr. Hills said to Earl. Then he turned to Eli. "What about your parents?"

Eli's shoulders slumped. "My parents…they…they died also." As he said it, he felt a searing pain in his heart. This was the first time he had ever lied. He wished the ground beneath his feet would open up so he could hide.

"Two orphans!" Mr. Hills boomed. "What a coincidence!" He turned to Elda, "Tell Lance to put up a notice around town tomorrow for runaway children. Let's see if anyone shows up to claim these two!"

"Yes, Papa," Elda answered, her eyes fixed on Eli. He saw mockery in her eyes.

Mr. Hills turned back to Eli and Earl. "In the meantime, you two will work in my restaurant. The money you earn will be used to pay off the debt you owe."

"Work?" Earl gasped as if Mr. Hills had just handed him a death sentence.

"OK," Eli agreed lightheartedly. He had been helping Mom with house chores since he was four years old. How hard could it be to work in a restaurant? Then the sparkle in his eyes dimmed as he remembered something. What about the missing jewels in his collar? What about the cure for the wolf kingdom?

"Mr. Hills," Eli asked, "how long do we have to work for you to pay off our debt?"

"Well, the only thing you two are qualified for is washing dishes. Let's see…" Mr. Hills rubbed his chin pensively. "I will pay you seven dollars and twenty-five cents an hour. You will work eight hours a day. I will provide you with three meals a day, but you must pay for your food at cost. At night, you can sleep on the kitchen floor for free."

Eli's head started to spin. He could not keep track of everything Mr. Hills had just said. He glanced at Earl, who was studying the ceiling while humming a soft tune of some sort. Apparently he had tuned out as well. The only person who was paying attention was Elda. While Mr. Hills talked, she punched numbers into a calculator.

Mr. Hills went on without missing a beat. "Our government will take a bunch of taxes out of your paycheck before the money gets to your hands. So net net, the two of you must work… Elda?"

On cue, Elda read a number off her calculator, "Sixteen and a half days!"

Sixteen and a half days? That's not so bad, Eli thought to himself. *My mission surely can wait sixteen and a half days.*

"OK, we will do it!" Eli piped up. Earl slumped to the floor.

"Good!" Mr. Hills leaned back in his chair. "Elda, show these gentlemen to the kitchen, please."

"Follow me." Elda walked out of the office. Eli put an arm under Earl and helped him to his feet. They followed Elda back through the narrow corridor into a brightly lit room.

CHAPTER 8

It's All Yours. Enjoy!

A dozen or so stoves were lined up against the windows. Dancing flames kissed steamy pots and pans. Five or six stout chimpanzees in white aprons and tall hats bustled about. Some were cooking at the stoves. Some were chopping and dicing at a workstation in the center of the room. One was scooping food onto large plates while yelling "Number three twenty-four is ready!" Lemur waiters threaded their way gingerly among workstations, stoves, and chefs, picking up prepared dishes or dropping off dirty plates.

Elda led Eli and Earl to a large sink in the corner. "Here you are, gentlemen." She gestured toward the sink as if she were unveiling the grandest gift in the world and said, "It's all yours. Enjoy!"

Eli and Earl looked at the sink. Dirty plates, bowls, and silverware were strewn everywhere. They overflowed onto the counter on both sides of the sink. Eli and Earl were standing in front of a mountain of dirty dishes.

"I can't breathe," Earl choked. Just then, a lemur waiter rushed in with a tray of dirty dishes.

"Richard," Elda called out, "meet our new dishwashing boys, Eli and Earl."

"Thank goodness you boys are here." Richard unloaded his tray onto Earl.

Crash! Plates smashed onto the floor into pieces. Earl collapsed like a sack of potatoes. The large tray slid from his limp hands.

"Earl!" Eli rushed forward and held Earl in his arms. Earl did not answer. He had passed out.

Don't miss the next
Enchanted Collar™ book,
in which Eli challenges grown-ups and
demands to be treated equally!

Enchanted Collar™ #3

Paradise Lost

Want more than just the stories?
Visit the *Enchanted Collar*™ website at
www.EnchantedCollar.com
See illustrations in full vivid color!
Get exciting sneak previews of the
next book! Watch videos and enjoy
other fun activities! And much more!

Connect with the author and other
Enchanted Collar™ fans
on FaceBook at
www.facebook.com/EnchantedCollar

Robin Y. Yang, MBA, CFA

is the author of the *Enchanted Collar*™ and *Economic Fairy Tales*™ series of books. She has been an investment analyst for thirteen years, during which she has published extensive investment research reports, been quoted in various publications, and delivered speeches at investment conferences.

After experiencing two major American financial crises, she started teaching children the basics of finance as a Junior Achievement volunteer. In 2011, she started writing the Enchanted Collar™ series and the Economic Fairy Tales™ series in her spare time to promote financial literacy among children and young adults.

Despite the fact that Ms. Yang used to wear a business suit and analyze dollars and cents on Wall Street, she remains a child at heart. Her favorite movies are animations. Wherever she travels, she makes a point to visit petting zoos, her favorite destinations. She lives and works in New York City.